Twinkle
Makes Music

by Katharine Holabird • illustrated by Sarah Warburton

Ready-to-Read

Simon Spotlight
New York   London   Toronto   Sydney   New Delhi

SIMON SPOTLIGHT
An imprint of Simon & Schuster Children's Publishing Division
1230 Avenue of the Americas, New York, New York 10020
This Simon Spotlight edition September 2022
Text copyright © 2022 by Katharine Holabird
Illustrations copyright © 2022 Sarah Warburton ·
Illustrations by Cherie Zamazing
All rights reserved, including the right of reproduction in whole or in part in any form.
SIMON SPOTLIGHT, READY-TO-READ, and colophon are registered trademarks of Simon & Schuster, Inc.
For information about special discounts for bulk purchases, please contact Simon & Schuster Special Sales at 1-866-506-1949 or business@simonandschuster.com.
Manufactured in the United States of America 0822 LAK
10 9 8 7 6 5 4 3 2 1
This book has been cataloged by the Library of Congress.
ISBN 978-1-5344-9677-4 (hc)
ISBN 978-1-5344-9676-7 (pbk)
ISBN 978-1-5344-9678-1 (ebook)

Twinkle woke up with a big smile.
Her wings glowed peachy pink.
She could not wait to go to school!
The fairies at The Fairy School
of Magic and Music were learning
how to play a special song.
Twinkle loved to make music
even though she often made mistakes!

But first, it was time
for some yummy breakfast.

"Good morning, forest friends,"
Twinkle said.
"Would you like to join me
for pinkberry tea and acorn muffins?"

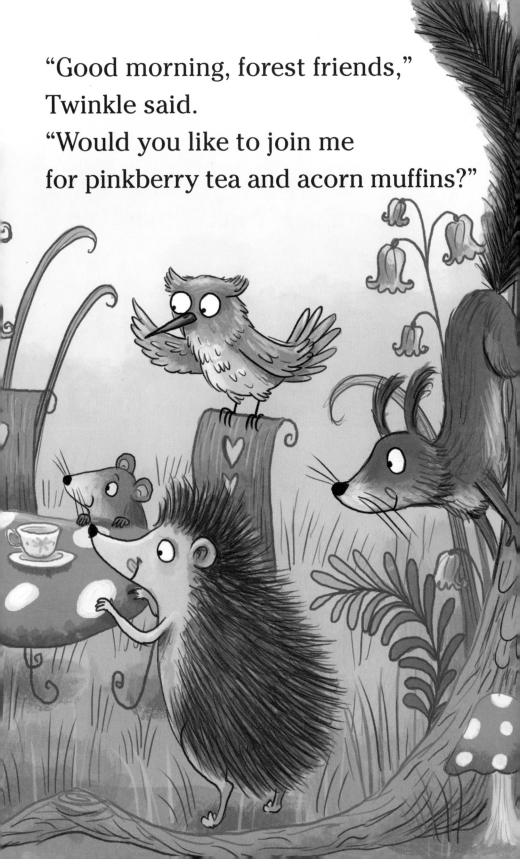

After breakfast Twinkle flew as fast
as her wings could go to school.
When she arrived, she sat next
to her friends Lulu and Pippa.
"Good morning, Twinks!" they said.

"We have an important visitor today,"
said their teacher, Miss Flutterbee.
Fairy Godmother smiled at the students.
"Hello, my little fairies," she said.
"I have a big announcement!"

"I am giving a special party
for all the hard-working musical fairies
at The Fairy School of Magic
and Music.
There will be delicious fairy treats
and lots of fun games and dancing.
As part of the celebration,
I would like you to perform
the special song you've been learning."

All the little fairies jumped for joy.
"You have all been practicing
well," said Miss Flutterbee.
"And I would like you
to continue playing music together
every day so that you are ready
for the big event."

"I can't wait to play the flute
at the party," Pippa said.
"I've been practicing every day!"
"Me too," Lulu agreed.

Twinkle also played the flute.
But even though she practiced a lot,
Twinkle's flute made strange noises!

"What am I going to do?"
Twinkle cried.
"I always make silly sounds
on the flute!"
"Don't worry, Twinkle,"
Pippa told her.
"We will practice with you."

"Absolutely!" Lulu said.
"We will play music together
after school, no problem!"

After school was over,
the three friends met
in the Sparkle Tree Forest.
"Ready?" asked Lulu and Pippa.
Twinkle nodded hopefully.

The fairies started to play. The sounds coming from Lulu and Pippa's flutes were sweet and musical.

But the only sounds that came from Twinkle's flute were funny whistles and squeaks!

"Spiders and bats!" Twinkle cried.
"What can I do?"
"Don't give up, Twinks," Pippa said.
"Okay," said Twinkle.
"I will keep trying.
Fairies never give up."

The next day,
after glitter painting,
fairy gymnastics,
and fairy-tale time,
the fairies lined up once again
for music class.

Twinkle took a deep breath
and blew as hard as she could
on her flute.

But no matter how hard she tried, the only sounds coming from her flute were more screeches and squeaks.

After class Twinkle was very unhappy.
Pippa and Lulu tried to cheer her up.
Miss Flutterbee kindly flew over.

"I cannot get the notes right,"
Twinkle admitted.
"I always try my very best,
but my silly music will ruin
Fairy Godmother's party!"

"Your music will not ruin the party,"
said Miss Flutterbee.
"Think about all the things you love
to do. And ask your forest friends
to help. There are many kinds of music
we can play."

Just then, they heard soft
twinkling sounds.
The fairies peeked around a tree.

Tweeter the bluebird was singing
a sweet birdsong.

Twinkle smiled. "That gives me
a great idea!" she said.
"I love to sing too, and I'll ask
all the forest creatures to join me.
We can all sing along with the music!"

"What a super idea!"
said Miss Flutterbee.

Twinkle flew into the forest,
waving her wand.
"Everyone, please come and join me
in the Forest Chorus!" she said.

Before long, all the creatures came
flying, running, and hopping to
join in Twinkle's musical chorus!

For the next two days, Pippa and Lulu
practiced playing their flutes
while Twinkle sang along,
and all the forest creatures sang
with her.
The music sounded better and better!

"I think we're getting the hang of it!"
Twinkle exclaimed.

Soon, it was the day of the party.
Twinkle arrived at Fairy Godmother's
palace surrounded by all the happy
forest creatures.
They were excited to join
in the musical chorus.

"Welcome, fairies and forest friends,"
Fairy Godmother announced.
"Today we celebrate the students of
The Fairy School of Magic and Music.
They will be playing a special song.
And Twinkle and the Forest Chorus
will sing along!

Then we will have some lovely treats,
and we will dance the fairy fandango,
and be very merry!"

The fairies began to play their flutes.
Twinkle took a deep breath
and began to sing,
and all the forest creatures joined
in the music.
It was a fairy-tastic concert!

When the music ended,
the fairies applauded
and cheered.
"Bravo!" Miss Flutterbee said.
"What a wonderful performance.
Thanks to all the musical fairies,
especially Twinkle and her
Forest Chorus!"
Lulu and Pippa gave Twinkle a big hug.
"We knew you would find a way!"
they said.
"Now, who wants fairy sparkle cake?"